Gary the Go-Cart

Carbon Comes out of the Closet

Written by BB Denson
Illustrated by Sidnei Marques

Desideramus Publishing - Houston, TX

Gary was a good go-cart.

He did as he was told.

He spent his days delivering

things that were bought and sold.

Gary and his sweet bird Sage
were dear things to behold.
Yet, their world would quickly change
as weird things would soon unfold.

Gary had his rituals.
He had his routines.
He would take the same trails.
He'd see splendid scenes.

Each day he'd pass apple trees
on his way to the mill.
He'd slow to smell the daisies
as he went down a hill.

He'd cruise past the cucumbers.
He loved to watch them grow.
Each day they got bigger till
their vines would overflow.

Then one evening on the news, the Greenies made their case; talking about carbon and how it was foul and base.

Let´s tax carbon...
Tax it now!
Soon everyone repeated,
"Your carbon is so bad.
Keep carbon in your closet,
every single bitty tad."
Clean Power is good!
Carbon is bad!

The politicians thought it clever.
They said, "For now and ever!"

"Sequester your carbon!
Your carbon cannot stray!
Sequester your carbon
and keep it all at bay!"

So Gary had to buy one,
and gizmos cost a lot!
Gary drained his piggy bank;
a gizmo he soon bought.

Gary had to hold his carbon till
he got home to his closet.

He had to hold it in until
he made the day's deposit.

Seems each time he stored carbon
it took more money too.
At this rate Gary thought soon
his dollars will be few.

Gary looked at the apples.
They didn't look so bad.
He asked them what they thought
and noticed they looked sad.

They told him they'd be bigger
if they had carbon galore.
Carbon is what they breathe in.
They simply needed more.

A cucumber then tells him
that carbon's going away.

Folks taking the carbon means
that puny they will stay.

"We are carbon-based life forms,
we need it to survive."

"All carbon's not pollution.
We need carbon to thrive."

Gary was a good go-cart.
He could not hurt those plants.
He had to do the right thing,
even if folks looked askance.

So Gary and Sage started spreading carbon all around.

They sprayed it in the air and scattered it on the ground.

The plants were all much healthier.
The plants were full of grins.

With carbon in the atmosphere
everybody wins.

Symbiosis at its finest.
Not like in the recent past.
The grass was now much greener.
The plants were growing fast.

For the Adults in the Room

"The unity of freedom has never relied on uniformity of opinion." **John F. Kennedy**

"From a quarter to half of Earth's vegetated lands has shown significant greening over the last 35 years largely due to rising levels of atmospheric carbon dioxide, according to a new study published in the journal Nature Climate Change." **NASA**

"The benefits of carbon dioxide supplementation on plant growth and production within the greenhouse environment have been well understood for many years."
Ontario Ministry of Agriculture, Food and Rural Affairs

"There are benefits to raising the CO2 level higher than the global average, up to 1500 ppm. With CO2 maintained at this level, yields can be increased by as much as 30%! Commercial greenhouses are aware of this and commonly use CO2 generators to maximize production."
Fifth Season Gardening Company

"Carbon dioxide is a powerful aerial fertilizer, directly enhancing the growth of almost all terrestrial plants and many aquatic plants as its atmospheric concentration rises." **Craig Idso, CO2 Science**

"The best estimate of CO2 concentration in the global atmosphere 540 million years ago is 7,000 ppm… As recently as 18,000 years ago, at the height of the most recent major glaciation, CO2 dipped to its lowest level in recorded history at 180 ppm, low enough to stunt plant growth. This is only 30 ppm above a level that would result in the death of plants due to CO2 starvation… The optimum level of CO2 for plant growth is between 1,000 ppm and 3,000 ppm in air, much higher than the 400 ppm in the global atmosphere today."
Dr. Patrick Moore, co-founder and former president of Greenpeace

"'Every great cause begins as a movement, becomes a business and eventually degenerates into a racket.' And those who benefit from the racket will defend it with passion."
Richard Lindzen quoting Eric Hoffer

"A lie gets halfway around the world before the truth has a chance to get its pants on."
Winston Churchill

Desideramus Publishing
Houston, TX
Desideramus.com

For information about custom editions, special sales and premium or corporate purchases, please contact Desideramus Publishing.

Note From the Author

Gary is a sentient, imaginary character. He emits CO2, which is the type of carbon that we are being told to sequester. Real vehicles emit a variety of gases, including both carbon dioxide and carbon monoxide. When I say carbon in this book, I am referring only to carbon dioxide. Since this is after all a children's book, I choose to simplify and just say "carbon". Please note that this book is not about carbon monoxide, which is indeed a pollutant. That is why in the book it clearly says, "All carbon's not pollutants".

I have had some people ask me about smog. Isn't that caused by carbon? Please know that there are various types of smog caused by a variety of sources, and include things like particulate matter, water vapor and a lot of different gases, mainly sulfur oxides and nitrogen oxides.

The point of this book is that carbon dioxide is natural and a very good thing.

Namaste

B.B. Denson

CPSIA information can be obtained at www.ICGtesting.com
Printed in the USA
BVIW12n0803190217
476579BV00009B/85